LOVING FORGIVENESS

By

Roben Oaktrey

Published by Young Oak Treasures 2024

TABLE OF CONTENTS

LOVING FORGIVENESS	1
TABLE OF CONTENTS	3
COPYRIGHT	5
SUMMARY	7
DEDICATION	9
INTRODUCTION	11
OUR DARK HOME	15
GHOSTS IN THE NIGHT	23
THE ATTIC	29
KATE'S PREDICAMENT	35
OUR NEW HOME	41
KRISTIN'S REVENGE	49
CIRCLE OF FRIENDS	59
ABOUT THE AUTHOR	65
ALSO BY ROBEN OAKTREY	67
DON'T MISS OUT!	69

COPYRIGHT

This is a work of fiction. Similarities to real people, places, or events are entirely coincidental.

LOVING FORGIVENESS

First edition. November 18, 2024.

Copyright © 2024 Roben Oaktrey.

Written by Roben Oaktrey.

SUMMARY

Matt and Marilou and their four children moved to their second home, in the heart of town. They left their cozy home in Wolf Hill Park to be closer to Matt's work; unaware of the effect this old, scary home would have on their family. The house appeared always dark, and everyone on the outside could hear the noises emanating from the inside. Every old house on the block had similar sounds, but their larger home manifested the loudest. Matt and Marilou, their children, and their neighbors ignored the scary noises emanating from all the surrounding homes. Nobody realized what would happen when they chose this course of action.

After one year, they moved to a house that was more centralized to Matt's work. They met new friends, and everything was fine until retribution from the old house took place on Gay's fourth birthday. Their family faced an important decision that would affect their futures and the futures of close friends.

Matt and Marilou and the children moved again to a home that was part of a circular neighborhood. They made new friends that lasted a lifetime.

DEDICATION

This book is dedicated to my grandchildren, Jose and Jenna.

INTRODUCTION

Our first home was in an established suburb called Wolf Hill Park. We lived within a few blocks of my dad's brother and sisters. My brother, sisters and I were all born while living in this house, and we always were at home and loved.

"Marilou, you now have four children. Are you going to stop or keep going?"

"Inez, I think I will stop at four, same as you. Elliot and Diedre will stop at their two. It is hard on Diedre having twins. This is always harder on the mother."

"Yes, I agree. I couldn't handle giving birth to more than one at a time. I think Charlotte will give it up. She and Will have been trying for a girl, and they are now happy with three boys. It looks like a girl is not in the cards for them."

"I love this neighborhood. However, Matt, being a builder, is getting the itch to move closer to town."

"Yes, Marilou, my husband Elliot, is the same way. I hope we all stick together, no matter where we go. I could not imagine living without being close to all of you."

"We all feel the same," said Charlotte.

We were all always getting together. Every Wednesday night, the parents would meet to play card games. The favorite one was canasta. They would have two tables going at the same time. All of us children would crawl around on the floor in contentment.

"Elliot and I have some news for everyone."

"Alright, Matt, what is the good news?" asked Uncle Mark.

"Marilou and I are planning to move closer to town."

"Because of my building business, Diedre and I are also planning to move closer to where the building is most popular right now."

"How soon will this take place?" asked Will.

"We will all be looking to sell our homes and

purchase other homes within a few weeks," said Marilou.

"This news is not so bad. We are all talking about moving soon. The only thing that stopped us is our friendship. Now that this is in the open, we can plan our move together. I understand Matt and Elliot must get going soon. The rest of us can enjoy a little more time to plan," said Charlotte.

"We will wait until you two settle in your new homes, and then we will get moving. We want us to stay close to each other. Besides, I don't want to find someone else to play canasta with," Will said, smiling.

Matt and Marilou, my parents, were the first to sell our home and move. They picked an old house in the west end part of town. This area had the most demand for new housing, because of the significant number of people moving from rural farms to cities. Mechanized farm equipment led to fewer jobs, and the growth of industrial opportunities created a need for workers.

OUR DARK HOME

We were the first of our four families to move to the city. My parents loaded us up in the car and drove us to see our next home for the first time.

"Children, here is our new home. Your mom and I hope you like it. We will move to another area in a year or two to get closer to my work."

"Where are all the other children?"

"Bobby, I am sure there are others. We will take walks around our new neighborhood and meet other nice people."

"Why is our home so dark?"

"Don't worry, Dawn. It is because the sun casts shadows on our home. Let's see what it looks like in the morning."

"Dad, I am scared. Will you stay with me?"

"Yes, Brian. I must go to work every day, but your mom will be with you. I will call and check in a few times during the day to make sure everyone is safe and sound."

The next day did not go as planned. The weather was overcast and our home still appeared to be dark and foreboding.

"Mom, the house is still dark on the outside. Why is it so dark inside also?"

"I am sorry, Dawn. It appears the weather is not cooperating with us. The paint on the inside could be a little lighter, which would help brighten things up a bit."

"Can we paint the inside?"

"Sorry, honey. We will move in a year or two and it would not be worth our time and expense to paint it. I hope it will be a suitable color for everyone until we move to our next home."

"It's fine with me. I hope the outside will get brighter. It seems so gloomy," said Bobby.

There seemed to always be a cloud over our home. The neighborhood walks, with the children, did not go as expected.

"Children, we are going to get dressed and take a walk today. I will push Gay in the stroller. The rest of you hold hands and stay with me. Bobby, you are the oldest at five. Make sure everyone holds hands and stays together."

During our walk through the neighborhood, we met several dogs and cats. A few people walked out to their front porch, then back into the house. We did not meet anyone. We also noticed something that was disturbing.

"Did anyone see our house is the darkest one in our neighborhood?"

"I am sure that is just an illusion. Why would our house be the darkest?"

"I don't know, but I think Bobby is right. The clouds over our house appear to be darker than in other areas."

"Now Dawn, let's not let our imagination run wild. I am sure we will meet some nice people soon, and all our fears will go away."

"I hope so. Why are so many noises outside during the night?"

"I am aware of these noises, too. Where are all the people talking at night, and why are there so many sirens?"

"Those are good questions, Bobby. I hope we meet some of our friendly neighbors who can give us answers."

We walked around our block for the rest of the week. At the end of the seventh day of walking, my mom started feeling uneasy. I noticed her spending a lot of time on the phone, talking with my dad. This made us lonely and uncomfortable.

"Thank you for calling me so many times today, Matt. I am paranoid about this house and the neighborhood."

"That is fine, Marilou. I will call as many times as necessary. The only problem is keeping a pocketful of change and having the time to drive to a pay phone. My business demands a lot of time on the road, but I can always stop and check in with you and the children. I can plan my day to be home in a few minutes if needed."

"I heard that. Thanks, Dad."

"You are welcome, Bobby. Now tell me about your walk today. Mommy says there are not any nice people out during the day?"

"Yes, she is right, Dad. Nobody talks to us. I hope that will change soon."

"School starts next week, and there should be lots of

children waiting for the bus. This will present an excellent opportunity to meet some new people."

My dad was correct. Starting mid week, we saw many children, with parents attending to them, waiting at the bus stops.

"Mom, there are lots of people out here now, with children. Can we try to meet some of them?"

"Yes, Bobby. We will start today."

My mom tried talking with several children and parents. They were all skeptical of us, since we were new to the neighborhood. Only one person talked to my mom.

"Hello, I am Marilou, and these are my children. We moved into your neighborhood just a few days ago."

"Yes, I have seen you walking the neighborhood. I am Kristin, and this is my three-year-old daughter, Kate. My ten-year-old son, Justin, is waiting for the bus. How do you like our neighborhood so far?"

"You are the first one to speak to us. Is everyone always so distant and unfriendly?"

"I assume the sirens and voices in the night got your attention?"

"Yes, we are hoping you can tell us what this is all

about?"

"This area of town comes to life after dark. The sirens are the police attending to calls of violence, vandalism, and theft. The people talking are your neighbors trying to find out what each other knows about the current events."

"Are we living in a dangerous part of town?"

"We all stick together and stay in touch. I will make sure you meet other neighbors and stay informed. How do you like your home?"

"It seems to be dark and intimidating."

"You are in a spot where there are lots of dense, tall trees. These provide a barrier to sunlight."

"Thank goodness. I hoped for a simple explanation. The children and I were becoming frightened. Did you all get that?"

"Yes, mom. Thank you, Miss Kristin," said Bobby.

Marilou, Kristin, and their children became great friends.

Kristin introduced Marilou to other adults in the neighborhood, which made everyone in the family comfortable with the outside area.

The inside of our home had noises of its own that

disturbed us.

GHOSTS IN THE NIGHT

My parents' honeymoon lasted throughout their marriage. They loved being together. We could not disturb them at night, unless it was an emergency. They left their bedroom open when we were little, but this changed to a door locked as time went by.

In order to make sure we did not disturb them, mom and dad told us of ghosts in the attic, and alligators under our beds. At night, the ghosts could come into our room if the closet doors were open or the door to the stairs to the attic was open or unlocked.

"I am glad mom and dad put all our beds in the same room, and we each have our own. We are close to each other and we can talk in a low voice so we do not disturb mom and dad."

"Me too, Bobby. I am too scared to be alone at night. If the closet door or the door to the attic stairs opened, my scream would wake the neighborhood. This is something we all know."

"Yes, you are right, Dawn. Once mom and dad tuck us in, I am not getting out of this bed until morning. Gay is lucky. She sleeps in a crib with side rails pulled up and the ghosts and alligators cannot get to her," said Brian.

Mom and Dad always tucked us in at bedtime. I wish they would have also said a prayer for us. We needed the extra protection.

"Good night kiddos."

"Good night mom and dad. Don't forget to make sure the closet door is closed."

"We will, Bobby."

"Don't forget about the door to the attic stairs and make sure you lock it. Please try to open it before you leave our room."

"We will, Dawn. Has everyone gone to the bathroom?"

When our parents tucked us in at night, we would always ask them to make sure the closet door was closed and the door to the attic stairs locked. If we had to go bathroom during the night - that was a problem for us.

We all developed habits of sleeping with our heads under the covers and keeping all our limbs on top of the bed. We did not want to go through life with only one hand or one foot.

One time, I remember, I had to go to the bathroom during the night. My brother and sisters never left their beds to go to the bathroom in that house. They wet the bed. My mom changed their sheets every day.

"Brian?"

"Yes, Bobby. What is it?"

"I have to go to the bathroom. Will you go with me?"

"No way. I am not leaving my bed. Can you just wet the bed like I do?"

"No, I cannot do that. Dawn, are you awake?"

"I am not going with you either."

"If we stay together and hold hands, then we will be stronger and the ghosts and alligators will not bother us."

"I am not going," said Dawn.

"Me neither," said Brian.

I laid there for what seemed like several hours, worrying about what to do. When I looked at my watch, the total lapsed time was about three minutes. I had to do something.

Our house did not have a basement. We had a crawlspace with the furnace under the floor. It is visible through the grate. When it came on, it glowed red and made loud screeching noises. My sisters and brother would not look at it.

"Dawn, can you hear the noise from the red thing beneath the floor? Mom and dad said it was the furnace."

"Yes, there is the red glow in the hallway."

"I will make my run for the bathroom when the furnace goes off."

"Bobby, don't go. You will get hurt. Stay in bed like us. I am afraid for you."

"Thank you, Dawn. I need to go. I am the oldest, and I need to be strong."

"Oh Bobby, you are going to die," Dawn said, crying.

"I will run fast."

After about five minutes, the furnace stopped, and the red glow faded away. Holding my breath, I jumped out of bed and ran toward the bathroom. The noises made me so scared; I was shaking.

I fell, and something wiggled all over my body.

"Dawn, come help me. The ghosts are all over me."

"I am too scared. Are you going to die? Get up and run."

"I can't. There are too many on me. I will try to crawl."

Creeping into the bathroom, I locked the door. When finished, I considered staying in the bathroom all night, but I ran back to my bed.

"Bobby, is that you? Are you alright?"

"Yes, Dawn. I am good. Once I made it to the bathroom, I realized the ghosts did not hurt me, and the alligators did not bite off my hand. I can do this all the time now. If you or Brian need to go to the bathroom, I will walk with you."

The next morning, I told mom what happened.

"Mom, I am getting bigger. I made it to the bathroom last night, and back into my bed without getting hurt. It felt like a lot of ghosts jumped on top of me, but I kept going. They do not bother me now."

"Yes, you are growing up, my little man. I am proud of you. You can help your brother and sisters."

Brian and Dawn never made it to the bathroom during the night while we lived in that house. Mom changed their sheets every day.

THE ATTIC

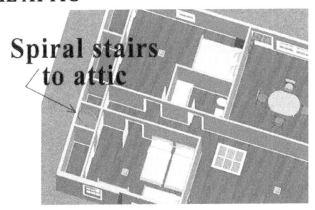

We used our attic for storage during the day, and the ghosts used it at night.

"Children, stay out of your bedrooms for a few hours. Dad and I will move some things we will not use right now into the attic."

"Will you close the door when you are not using the stairs?"

"I am sorry, Dawn. The door will remain open, since we will go up and down carrying items for storage."

"I am not going near our bedroom with that door open. Please let me know when you lock it."

"Sounds good, Brian. I will let you know."

Our parents talked while moving items to the attic. The idea of moving close to that open door with the stairway to doom scared us.

"Dawn, are mom and dad talking in the attic?"

"Yes, Bobby. I am glad you said that. It almost sounded like ghosts."

"Matt, do you think we have enough room for everything up here?"

"I believe so. I am trying to leave a path so we can get to our things with ease."

"That is a great idea. I will help. We also need to limit our time doing this. We should spend more time with our children and let them help us whenever it is possible and safe for them."

"I agree. Let's constrain our time in the attic to one hour per day. That should be ample time for us and the children."

"I am glad there is a window at each end and one in the front. This lets light and fresh air into our attic."

"I agree. Time is up. Let's get downstairs with the children."

After locking the door to the attic, Matt and Marilou took the children out for a walk around the neighborhood.

"Who is up for a walk around the block?"

"We are always ready for a walk, Dad. Is mom coming too?"

"Yes, mom is also coming. She loves walking together."

"Dad, will the sounds from our house be loud when we are outside?"

"Let's walk outside and find out."

We all walked outside and listened for the scary sounds.

"The sounds are coming from our house. These will continue all the time. Don't let these noises from outside scare you. We will ignore these and enjoy our walk. The sounds will diminish the farther away we are from home."

"Thank you, Dad. The noises from our furnace and the other sounds coming from the walls and attic are going away as we walk. I was worried these sounds would follow us. I feel much better now, and I can ignore these."

"You are welcome, Dawn. There is nothing to fear. Those are just normal noises in every house. Everything is fine, and we can choose to ignore these sounds."

We continued our walk in peace, ignoring the sounds coming from our house and other houses in the neighborhood.

"Hello Kristin. How are you, Kate, and Justin doing today?"

"We are doing great, Marilou. Thank you for asking."

"We are glad to get away from the noises of our home. It scares the children, and sometimes me, too. I noticed these houses have noises of their own."

"Yes, we all had the same company install our furnace and water heater. The noises seem to travel inside the walls, under the floor and into the attic."

"Our house seems to be the loudest."

"That is because your home is one of the largest, with larger appliances."

"I guess so. It is good to see you. Would you like to join us on our walk today?"

"Sorry, I must work on cleaning my house today. I will not have time for a walk, only to check the mail."

We stayed in that house for a little over one year. We adjusted to the sounds, both inside and outside.

Ignoring these seemed to be the best plan.

KATE'S PREDICAMENT

We started playing outside, in our yard with friends, after about 3 months.

"I am so glad you to are ready to play outside. It has been lonely out here without you."

"We are not as old as you are, Bobby. You also can go to the bathroom during the night. We still can not do that. Brian will not budge from his bed at night. It does not matter if all doors are closed, and the furnace is off. He is afraid of the alligators and ghosts. The only reason he is out here with us now is he is afraid to stay inside the house without one of us there with him. He is still afraid of the noises we hear outside."

"He needs to ignore those sounds, like dad told us. It makes things so much easier."

"You are right. He is younger than us. Brian will get it some day, if we are here long enough," said Dawn.

"Here comes Kate. She lives next door, and it is easy for her to come into our yard and play with us."

"Hi Kate."

"Hi Dawn. The noises coming from your house are much louder than those coming from my house. Does it hurt your ears?"

"We have learned to ignore those sounds. It makes things much easier."

"I will try to do that. It may take me a while."

We all played together and had lots of fun for several months.

"Children, the day is here. This house is now sold, and it is time to move to our new home, closer to your father's work. We have about two weeks to get out of this house. Your dad rented a moving van for two weeks. When we finish loading it up, we will drive it to our new home. Let's pack tomorrow."

"We need to tell our friends. Did you inform Miss Kristin?" asked Dawn.

"Yes, I called her today and let her know. She will

miss us all and we will miss her, too. "

We spent the rest of the day talking with our friends. There was lots of crying from all of us. Kristen let her children stay with us as much as possible during the next two weeks. Our parents saved moving the items from the attic for the last.

"Children, we are saving the attic for last. The door to the stairway will stay locked until we have everything else out of the house and into the moving truck. Your father and I will then unlock the door and bring everything from the attic and load it into the truck."

"When can we see our new home?"

"Dawn, we do not have time now to show you. Let's get this truck loaded, and then we will all drive there together and move in."

"Sounds good to me. Bobby, and Brian, we all need to get everything out of our bedroom and carry it to the van. Mom or dad will help us with the beds. I am glad we kept all our clothes in our parent's bedroom. In our new home, mom said we will have a chest of drawers to hold our clothes."

We all worked hard. After thirteen days, we finished all loading and cleaning up the house. It was now mom's and dad's turn to clean out the attic.

"Children, play outside for a couple of hours while we clean out the attic. We will monitor you, don't worry. Remember to ignore the noises from the house. We will lock the door when we finish."

"Gay has it easy. She just sits there and, after a few minutes, falls asleep. I think we should all stay close to the house."

"Sounds good, Dawn. Has anyone seen Kate? It is time for her to come and play with us."

"She must be in her house taking a nap or eating a meal. It would be nice to say goodbye to her."

Mom and dad came out to tell us they finished, and it is time to go to our new house.

"We finished packing. It is time to go to our new home. Everybody ready to go?"

"Yes, we are. Gay is sound asleep."

Dad picked up Gay, and the rest of us headed to the car. He drove the moving van, and mom drove us in our car. The work truck is at our new house. Before we left, Kristin came over to say goodbye.

"Wait a minute, please. Has anyone seen Kate?"

"I don't think so. Should we stop and help you look for her?"

"No, Marilou, thank you. I am sure she is somewhere close."

We all noticed the noises coming from our house, and thank goodness we learned to ignore these. Miss Kristin also ignored the familiar noises. After a few days, we wanted to go back and see our old house one more time.

"Mom, can we go back to our old house for another look?"

"Sure, Dawn. Everyone hop into the car."

"I can tell when we get close. The screeching and crying noise of our furnace gets louder."

"Yes, Dawn, these sounds used to make us scared."

"You are right, Bobby. Let's drive around the block a few more times before we return home. Matt, stop for a minute. What is that?"

Firetrucks, police and an ambulance were all converging on our old home. My dad drove up, and we all got out of the car to see what was going on.

"There they are! Those children ignored the noises coming from their house."

"Yes, that is true. We all learned to ignore the scary noises of our house and the others," said Bobby.

"When you cleaned out your house, my daughter climbed the stairs to your attic. When she tried to leave, she could not open the locked door for three days. I thought she might be up there, and I called the police to come and open the door."

"Oh, my goodness. She must have climbed into the attic after we finished. We did not know she was up there. Is she alright?" asked my mom.

"Yes, she appears to be hungry and thirsty. Your children should have paid attention to her crying."

"Don't blame my children. You also could have noticed the crying. This is an accident, and it is a true blessing that she is not hurt. You need to be thankful, instead of looking for blame. All of us are to blame for not listening to the noises."

Kate's mother hated us for not helping her child. Kristin plotted and waited for the right time to hurt our family.

OUR NEW HOME

It was a joyful day when my dad sold our house and we moved to an area called Pike's Trace. We moved into a house similar to the one we had in Wolf Hill Park.

"Dad, how long are we going to be in this house?"

"Only a couple months, Bobby. The people who sold us their home need a little more time to get everything moved out."

"Are there ghosts in the closet and alligators under our beds?"

"Sorry, Dawn, we are not sure. Just to be safe, do not get out of the beds during the night."

"Thank you, mom. Don't worry, we won't. Don't forget the rubber sheets, just in case."

"I will not get out of my bed until morning. I don't want to take any chances."

"Yes, Brian, we understand. I will get up and go to the bathroom. I am getting bigger and I am not scared anymore."

We kept most of our things in boxes. The two months went by fast, and we prepared to move into our new home again.

"Let's pack everything up and into the truck. Everybody knows the drill. The only difference is we do not worry about scary sounds and keeping the attic door locked."

"We got it, mom. When we finish loading up, let's all take a walk through every inch of the house. We do not want a repeat of what happened to Kate."

"I agree, Bobby. That is a good point. We will all make sure we left nothing behind, including any small children or animals that may wander into the house without us seeing them."

The truck is now loaded again, and the last walk through is complete.

"Let's do this one more time. Everyone get into the car as we head to our new home. Should only take about 5 minutes to get there."

"Thanks, Dad. We are all ready to go. I made sure nobody is in the house."

"Thank you, Bobby."

The drive was very short. We loved the sight of our new home. It was a one-story, with Bedford stone all around, a huge driveway that sloped to the street, a full basement, and a fenced backyard.

"Our new house is beautiful! Thank you, mom and dad."

"You are welcome, Dawn. There should be lots of children for you all to play with. The school is just across the street. There is also another school, and a small shopping center, about two blocks in the other direction."

"I can see other children our age walking around. They seem curious to see their new neighbors."

"I see them too," said Brian.

"Mom, are there ghosts in the closet and alligators under the bed in this house?"

"No, Dawn, there are not. This house is empty of ghosts and alligators. However, always be careful getting up during the night to go to the bathroom. We don't want anybody to get hurt falling down, or any other injuries."

"I am still not getting out of my bed during the night, and the closet door stays closed. I want to be the first one to ride my pedal car down the driveway."

"Sounds great, Brian. I want to be second, with my bicycle," said Bobby.

"I will be next on my girl's bicycle," said Dawn.

During our first year in this home, we all met new friends, including mom and dad.

"Matt, I met a new friend. Her name is Christy, and her husband is Kendall. I think you will like her husband. They also have a son, Steve, who is Dawn's age, but he may be a better friend to Bobby, since he is a boy."

"Sounds good, Marilou. I can be friends with anyone. I am sure he is a fine man. Let's set up a time to play cards with them. Do they know how to play canasta?"

"Yes, they do. I will call today and set it up. How does every Wednesday evening sound? We will take turns hosting. The kids could play together, just as we did in Wolf Hill Park."

"Sounds great. I am looking forward to it."

We visited with our next-door neighbors, the Osbornes. They always gave us cookies and milk.

"Hi Mr. and Mrs. Osborne. How are you today?"

"Well, hello there, Bobby. I am doing fine. How are your mom and dad?"

"They are doing fine, thank you."

"Here are a few cookies and some milk from Mrs. Osborne. Have you started school?"

"No, not yet. My mom said I do not have to go to kindergarten. I am waiting for first grade."

"That sounds like a challenge. Are you ready for that?"

"My mom has been teaching me to read and write. She says I will be ready."

"That is good. Please stop by often to say hello to us. Please ask your brother and sisters to stop by anytime. We love visiting with all of you. God bless you."

Sometimes, the Sterns invited us to their house to make delicious homemade ice cream.

"I get to turn the crank first!"

"You were first last time, Bobby. It is my turn to go first."

"You are right, Dawn. It is your turn."

After our first year in this house, I started first grade, and my sister Dawn started kindergarten. A girl living across the street, in the 5th grade, walked us to school and took us home every day.

"Hurry Bobby and Dawn. Janie is waiting for you."

"We are on our way," said Dawn.

"Bobby and Dawn, listen to me. You will both hold hands and one of you will hold my hand. We will stay like this all the way to school and back home. Always listen to me. There are cars coming and going, and we want nothing to happen to any of us."

We always listened to her, and nothing ever happened. We were always safe with Janie. The next year, during Christmas, we welcomed a visitor into our home.

"Children, let's all go down to the basement. There is a surprise for you."

"Baby chickens! This is wonderful! Thank you, mom and dad."

"You are all welcome. Now be careful with these. They are delicate, just as when you were a baby."

"What was that sound?"

Dad seldom asks us that question.

"I think it is bells and some stomping, like something is on the roof."

"That is what I thought, Bobby. Do you notice anything else?"

We all stood silent and listening. We heard something that surprised us.

"HO HO HO. Merry Christmas!"

Is it him? We all looked at the top of our basement stairs.

"Santa! It is Santa!," we all exclaimed.

Santa walked down our basement stairs carrying a large bag over his shoulder. We were all so excited, we could pop. Mom and dad stood there, smiling and crying. Santa handed out the toys we always wanted, and then he smiled at mom and dad and said he must be going because he had other stops to make.

We all stood there smiling and crying in amazement. When Santa got to the top of the stairs, I did something quick.

"Mom and Dad, I am going to see Santa's sled and reindeer. I will be right back."

I ran upstairs and outside as fast as I could. Santa had already left.

"How did he leave so fast?"

"Because he is Santa, son. He is magic."

I let it go, and we all played with our toys and had the best Christmas ever.

The next month, something unexpected happened to our family.

KRISTIN'S REVENGE

We had a wonderful Christmas at our house. We all enjoyed playing with our new toys, and mom and dad enjoyed the peace; until Brian got a little careless.

"This is so good, Marilou. The kids are content and playing with their new toys. We can now enjoy a little time to talk to each other."

"Yes, it is nice. Are you enjoying the card games with Christy and Kendall? They both seem to enjoy it when we are together."

"Kendall and I get along great. He has a good sense of humor and a good head for business. We exchange ideas and respect each other's opinions. His son, Steve, seems to get along great with our children."

"Steve is a good friend to our children. We are so blessed."

"There goes Brian. He enjoys that new pedal tractor."

"He sure does. I just wish he would not ride it in the middle of the street."

The unexpected happened.

"Oh, my goodness. Matt, come with me quick. A car hit Brian and he is laying in the street."

"I am so sorry. I did not see him. He ran his tractor right in front of my car. Is he alright?"

"Brian, honey, can you sit up?"

"Yes, mommy, I am not hurt. His car hit my tractor and knocked it over."

"We are taking you to the hospital just to make sure."

"I will get the car, Marilou. You stay here with Brian."

Mom and dad lifted Brian into the car and drove to the hospital. The man who hit him left his contact information and phone number for his insurance. They did not complete their trip to the hospital.

"Brian, are you sure you are alright?"

"Yes, mommy. I don't want to go to the hospital. I am afraid of what they will do to me and I am not injured."

"Matt, what do you think? Maybe Brian is right. I think he remembers when we took him to the hospital and they pumped his stomach after he ate some mothballs. I don't want to put him through any unnecessary trauma."

"Let's go home and we will check him out and watch him overnight. If anything seems out of the ordinary, we will take him to the hospital right away."

"That sounds like a good plan. Brian, is this alright with you? Tell us if you are hurting anywhere on your body, and if you are sick, or like something is wrong."

"I will, mom. Thank you for not taking me to the hospital. I dislike the things they do to me."

Mom and dad took Brian back home. Dad called the man who hit Brian. He thanked him and told him everything was alright, and Brian appears not injured. The considerate man called us after a week to check on Brian.

"We made it through another emergency. Hopefully, there won't be any more."

"I hope not, Marilou. We are young, but things like this put age on us. We got over Dawn being run over by a bicycle, and Brian's episode with the mothballs. My goodness, I hope there are not any other incidents."

"Gay's fourth birthday is coming up soon. We should call and invite everyone over for her party. Let's also invite Christy, Kendall and Steve."

"That is a good idea. We have a couple of months to get it together."

Mom and dad set up Gay's fourth birthday party. Everyone came and had a wonderful time.

"It is always good visiting with family and friends that we have not seen for a while. Kendall and Christy and Steve made a pleasant addition to the family. Matt, they are a blessing to us."

"I am thankful, Marilou. We had no episodes."

The next week, something unexpected happened.

"The children are out back, in our fenced yard, playing. Matt, can you come here and look at a problem with the kitchen sink?"

"What is the problem with it?"

"It is not draining good. Can you fix it or should we

call a plumber?"

"I will give it a shot. All I need to do is to disconnect the trap, and see what the problem is. I will do this right now."

"Wait a minute, Matt. Where is Gay?"

"What do you mean, Marilou? She is in our fenced backyard, playing. I am going to call Christy and Kendall to come down and help look for her."

All the neighbors looked for Gay and could not find her.

"I am calling the police."

"Good idea, Marilou. We should not wait any longer."

The police came, took the report, and started looking right away. Their guess was she may have stepped into a hole. Mom cried and shook, and Dad was not much better.

"We will do all we can to find your daughter. Our policy is to stay in touch, and you may call us at anytime. I am hoping she will turn up soon, and be all dirty from falling in a hole and scrambling to get out."

"Thank you, officer. Please stay in touch with us. Matt and I will do our own search and stay in touch with you. Our wonderful neighbors will help us. We are so blessed."

"Marilou, it is getting late. We should get some rest. You and I can sleep in shifts. I will stay awake the first half of the night, and then you can stay awake while I try to sleep. Our baby is out there somewhere and we will find her. God will help us. I have faith he will take charge at any moment."

"Thank you, Matt. I will try to get some sleep, but I cannot guarantee it."

The next day, Gay is still missing.

"My little baby. She is only four years old. How is she going to make it without us? Matt, is there anything else we can do?"

"We can pray and ask our friends to do the same."

On the third day, there are results in the search.

"Marilou, I have an idea. We need to get the police to check every house around us. She could not have gone far. They can break into houses that are vacant. I will get this started."

"Thank you Matt. Let's pray for results."

The police went into action. They knocked on doors, and if nobody answered, they broke the door down.

"The phone is ringing. I need to get it."

"Hello Ms. Marilou? This is the police. We found your daughter. Please come to this address. We have some questions for you and your husband while your daughter is telling us what happened."

"Matt, let's go. The address is a vacant house right around the corner."

Mom and dad loaded us into the car and we drove to the vacant house where the police found Gay.

"There are a lot of police cars here. Why is Ms. Kristin in handcuffs?"

"I don't know, Bobby. We will find out soon. Let's go Matt. Children, come with us and stay close."

"Gay! Are you alright, honey? How did you get into this empty house?"

"It is alright, Mommy. I knew someone would come soon. There was plenty of food and water, and blankets, and this did not scare me. Ms. Kristin took good care of me and she told me not to worry."

"Officer, what are the plans for Kristin?"

"She is guilty of kidnapping and other charges involving child endangerment. She could face several years in prison. Her child will go into the foster care system until she gets out of prison."

"Please do not do this to Ms. Kristin. She did not hurt me, and she was very kind and protective."

"Officer, my husband and I and our children would like to have a private conversation with Kristin."

The police stepped away while the conversation between Kristin, Marilou, Matt, and their children took place.

"Kristin, what were you thinking? You may leave Kate for several years. Why did you do this?"

"You are right, Marilou. Revenge was on my mind. I wanted you to feel what I did when Kate could not get out of your attic for three days. I waited until Gay was four years old, as Kate was when she was in this same predicament. The only difference, is I made sure Gay was safe, warm, and had plenty of food and water. My Kate had none of these things. I love my daughter, as you do yours, and I am glad you found Gay. She is a wonderful person, and worthy of all the love she can get."

"Mommy, I can see why Ms. Kristin did this. I am only four years old, and I can see she loves her daughter very much, as you love me. Please help her. I feel she loves me, too."

"You are right, sweetheart. We all have been through a lot, including Ms. Kristin. We all deserve second chances. Officer, please release Kristin. We do not want to press any charges. We have all suffered enough."

"Please do as my wife said. We do not want to press any charges against Kristin. Thank you for your help."

They released Kristin, and no charges filed against her. We did not see or hear from Kristin again.

"Our neighbors must think we are crazy for not pressing charges."

"Let them think what they want, Marilou. We did the right thing, and we all stuck together. Gay is fine and healthy. Our little girl is also very smart. Our family learned a lot from her tonight. Thank you, Jesus, for the gift of loving forgiveness."

We stayed in this house for about three years.

CIRCLE OF FRIENDS

We sold this house and moved to one that was in a perfect location for my dad's work. Our relatives also moved close to us. This house was in a circular neighborhood. There was a large home in the middle of the circle with a pool. We also had a pool. All the children were the same age as us, and we developed close friendships that lasted a long time after school.

"Mom, how long will we stay in this house?"

"Dawn, we do not have any plans to move. We will be here for a long time."

"That is good. Now we can make friends and play together without fear of leaving. Are there any ghosts in our closets and alligators under the beds?"

"No, sweetheart. You don't have to worry about

that any longer."

"I am still not going to the bathroom during the night and my closet door stays closed," said Brian.

"I already have friends at the end of the street. We plan to play monopoly together. One boy is my age and we are in the same classes at school. His brother is only a year older, and he plays with us, too. They have nine children; seven boys and two girls."

"That is great, Bobby. Brian, how are you doing with friends?"

"I am doing fine. There are a few boys a couple of houses down the street and we like to play with our plastic army men and our little cars and trucks. I love this neighborhood."

"Don't forget, Aunt Inez and Uncle Mark and their children are just a block away. You can always play with them any time."

"Thanks, Dad. Can we invite any of the neighbors over to swim in our pool?"

"Let's give that some time, Bobby. Our family, including Kendall, Christy, and Steve, will come over for birthdays and holidays. Our pool will get a lot of use without overdoing it."

We stayed in this house for over nine years. There

were lots of children our age, and we made a lifetime of wonderful memories.

Kendall and Christy stayed best friends with my mom and dad as long as they lived.

I visited this house about sixty years later. The current owners welcomed me into their house and showed me around. Lewis and Jennifer remembered my parents and asked about them. Lewis showed me where he did some remodeling of the back room. He also showed the pool, and they will fill it in the next day. It had a leak that was too expensive to fix. All their children and grandchildren were older now and did not take the time to swim in the pool.

"Hello Bobby. Please come in and I will show you around your old house. You might like to see the changes we made. I believe your parents were Matt and Marilou?"

"Yes, you are correct. Did you know my parents?"

"Several people in the neighborhood remember them. They told us what wonderful people they were, and your dad built this room on the back."

"Yes, I remember that."

"I removed the roof system and replaced it with roof trusses with a low pitch to keep the water off."

"That is a great idea. I remember there were a few small leaks that never stopped. That is a problem with flat roofs."

"Here is the pool. Sorry, you are seeing it for the last time. Our children and grandchildren are all older now and have no interest in swimming in our pool. There is also a leak that is too expensive to fix. We are filling in the pool tomorrow."

"Are there any people still living in this neighborhood that were here during our time?"

"Little Joe returned from his term in the Army. He met a nice young lady and they married. Soon after their marriage, they bought the house on the other side of the circle. Walk with me to the front yard and I will show you."

"Thank you, Lewis. I remember him well, and the day he left for the service. Our neighborhood had a going away party for him. He was a good friend to all of us."

"There is the house. His red pickup truck is in the driveway. He is the only one from your generation who returned to the neighborhood. He retired last year and stays to himself. His wife, Sharon, walks the circle alone. She is friendly and always tells us she will tell Joe we said hello. You might see her when you leave today."

"I must be going. Thank you, Lewis, for the tour. It

is a pleasure meeting you and Jennifer."

As I was leaving the neighborhood, I saw a lady walking around the circle.

"Hello, are you Sharon, Joe's wife?"

"Yes, I am. Are you a friend of Joe's?"

"We were friends when he was much younger and lived in the house in the middle of the circle. He was a wonderful friend to all of us. How is Joe?"

"He is doing fine. Since he retired, he doesn't get out much. The neighborhood has changed so much, it depresses Joe. There are no more block parties, and everyone sticks to themselves. Joe misses the old neighborhood."

"Please tell Joe I said hello. I will stop by again."

I did not return to the old neighborhood. Joe died a few weeks later. Sharon reported in his obituary he had a sudden illness that took his life in a short period.

None of us visited our home in the West End. We heard someone demolished it to make room for apartments.

We all had a wonderful life. Thank you, Jesus.

***

ABOUT THE AUTHOR

Roben Oaktrey is the author of several short stories, including three in the Hailey series: First Show with Buddy; Buddy's Last Show; and First Show with Dusty.

Roben has participated in several adventurous activities throughout his life, and is now a retired construction engineer.

He spends most of his time with his grandchildren and writing short stories.

Read more at https://Robenoaktrey.com

ALSO BY ROBEN OAKTREY

Hailey
Hailey: First Show With Buddy
Hailey: Buddy's Last Show
Hailey: First Show With Dusty

Timely Relationships
Timely Relationships: A New Beginning
Timely Relationships: 1855 Wild West
Timely Relationships: 1980 Rescue

Standalone
Grandparents Parenting: Joys and Rewards
Graham Crackers
Larie
Life Happenings of Reave Kaasterman
Tales From An Old Framing Carpenter
Confrontations
My Warmhearted Son
Without Merit
General's Flowers

Watch for more at https://Robenoaktrey.com

DON'T MISS OUT!

Sign up to receive emails whenever Roben Oaktrey publishes a new book. There's no charge and no obligation.

https://books2read.com/r/B-A-XFPN-ARHPB

Connecting independent readers to independent writers.

* * *

www.ingramcontent.com/pod-product-compliance
Ingram Content Group UK Ltd.
Pitfield, Milton Keynes, MK11 3LW, UK
UKHW042047131224
452457UK00001B/53